THE BOLEY TWINS

A Ghost Story

J. TURBERVILLE

The Boley Twins

Copyright © 2025 J. Turberville

ISBN (Paperback): 979-8-89672-159-8
ISBN (Hardback): 979-8-89672-160-4
ISBN (Ebook): 979-8-89672-161-1

Because of the dynamic nature of the Internet, any
web addresses or links contained in this book may
have changed since publication and may no longer
be valid. The views expressed in the work are solely
those of the author and do not necessarily reflect
the views of the publisher, and the publisher hereby
disclaims any responsibility for them.

Printed in the United States of America.

PROMINENT
BOOKS
EDGE

5830 E 2nd St, Ste 7000 #9983
Casper, WY 82609
USA

To my Aunt Tina.
Your bit of color has been missed.

THE TWINS ARRIVE

The ghost of the young girl was watching Miranda and her brother when they arrived at the home of Aunt Eloise during that steamy summer of 1901. Miranda thought she had a tragic death and could sense the smell of burnt flesh. The big old house of Aunt Eloise was just a block from the library and the train station. The ancient Magnolia tree covered the entire right side of the yard from the ground to the sky. The deep porch looked across at the smaller homes across the street. Of course the ceiling was painted sky blue to confuse the wasps. The small town by the river was beautiful. The new courthouse on the square and the gaily decorated shops rung of happiness. The town of Sugar Lot was a lot of evil and not of sugar. She watched the ladies of the town planting flowers at the base of the statue of a civil war soldier. She did notice it faced south. She also saw the shadow of the soldier as he watched the women. He slowly turned in her direction and almost waved as he was so surprised to see that she could actually see him. He paused but a moment and then turned his attention back to the Confederate Jasmine.

Their mother had sensed the danger which was coming their way. She had hoped sending them to her home town would keep them safe. She had been surrounding them with the protection of her love but realized they would have to create their own place of self. She could not admit what was. Their mother had also seen things as a child but had built a protective wall for her sanity. Her daughter would prove to be stronger and her twin brother, John Michael, was able to channel energy for both their protection. In an earlier time he would have been called a witch. Miranda was a medium of some power. Their aunt and uncle acknowledged their gifts and were comfortable around them as long as they could not see the shadows. Aunt Eloise did not possess the gift and for that she was forever thankful.

As they approached the house a coffin was coming from the front door beneath the gingerbread trim. It was a dark oak with brass handles that sparkled in the sun. Suddenly it was gone as Miranda glanced at John Michael. Aunt Eloise came rushing out the door like the gust of wind she was. "Sweet children", she said, as she bent down and pressed them into her breasts. "How is that crazy mother of yours who finally let you come visit?" "Your uncle Charles cannot wait to share the summer with you two."

In the distance they could see the dark ones. These were entities Miranda referred to as the watchers. They had no influence over events as a rule but were drawn to places of the living. They were pitiful to see and hear. Their wailing was like a headache in the back of the head. Miranda could easily block them out but they made John Michael weary when they came about. These shadows seemed to be determined by the darkness of their forms. Those which were blacker than black were the stronger and the ones to avoid. They would pull you into their circle of influence and could cause harm. These were the souls of the damned who would forever walk the earth. Those of the lightest shades were but memories. They were the holders of events which were traumatic while they lived. Over time most would dissipate. They just gave a glimpse of what once was. The gray colors were the true ghosts who had yet to move into the light to another plane. Often they would show their true forms as they tried to share their stories.

Miranda made note of the children playing jump rope as she walked towards the house, They were singing, "The doctor sang touch your toe and now slap your head. Sing a song of darkness as you will soon be dead. Go into the kitchen and bring out the leaven bread. Give it to the sin eater to make the soul well. Then get under the covers to protect yourself from hell." John Michael was wondering what piece of history had lead to the rhyme. It seemed obvious that the children attached no importance to the chant.

As they entered the house they could see the lady sitting in the coffin in the main parlor. They nodded towards her as she winked at them. This was the spirit of their grandmother, Lilith, who often came to give them direction for their psychic gifts. As animated as she appeared this was going to be an interesting summer. Each time she appeared was a warning of more things to come. They were surprised to see the cat sitting in her lap. She was drawn a bit to be dramatic She just loved to pose with the casket. Aunt Eloise always said it was a good thing she could not see her mother. She would have to chase her and that damn coffin out of the parlor. Who ever heard of a self respecting ghost riding everywhere in a coffin?

As they were unpacking in their rooms they heard a commotion of horse and wagon racing into the drive. Suddenly Mr. Malone, the ice man, was at the door calling for the doctor. Running from his office on the side of the house Uncle Charles was suddenly outside. "Doctor", he screamed with concern in his voice, "Old lady Wilson is dead. I delivered ice and found her in her kitchen chair. Come quick." She lived just across and road and down the street a bit so off they raced. Naturally the twins were right behind and soon they were in front of the small shotgun house. The two men raced into the kitchen were Uncle Charles determined she had recently died. The corpse was limp and there was a faint smile on her lips. Her cup of coffee was still warm with steam rising to the ceiling. Yes, she had had a peaceful passing.

The children immediately saw the spirit of Mrs. Wilson sitting in the rocking chair on her porch. She was looking into the distance and made no acknowledgement of seeing them. She was watching her husband who had passed 40 years earlier. He was walking down the road towards the house. He was young and had a spring in his step. He was whistling that same tune that used to drive her crazy. My how she had missed hearing the dull tune. He had been waiting for her but was late for her passing. He had gone first to the house where he died all those years ago. But for a moment of time he revisited his death and immediately came for his wife.

She watched in despair as he approached not realizing she had been transformed into the appearance of the young woman she once was. Miranda was observing her change down to a dress of an earlier time. My what a beauty she had been. Widow Wilson's husband walked onto the porch, nodded at Miranda and embraced the spirit of his wife. They turned towards Miranda and John Michael with a smile of contentment and drifted into the light. All that was left was the gentle rocking of her chair. The ice man noticed this rocking and crossed himself as he pointed at the chair. He had suddenly turned quite pale and called out to the Virgin Mother to protect him from the spirits. Covering the front door was the black form of a long and thin shadow which did not belong at the scene of this death. It was holding a bowler hat which he moved from hand to hand. He looked almost nervous as he eyed the twins. Several other shadow forms were with him and they evoked such a strong emotion of sorrow that Miranda began to weep. She could sense they were trying to ask her for help when the dark one abruptly disappeared. Miranda would have to ponder him another time.

Uncle Charles told the children to run back home and he would be along after the body was removed. Aunt Ruth was putting supper on the table as the children entered the house, "Go wash your face and hands and come to eat."

Crossing the front parlor they found Lilith sitting in the wingback chair observing them. "Children, how you have grown. How is your mother? You know she hides from her gifts and will not let me in her home. I see you witnessed that dark shade at the home of that widow. Avoid him in the future as long as you can. He is but the edge of evil coming to this town. You will need to be strong and confident. He is called the collector. He captures souls of the dead to stop them from entering the afterlife, This gives him power. The more he collects the more he can influence the living. He is but the forefront of a force coming this way. A force only the two of you will be able to stop." And then she was gone. It always got under the skin of the twins that Lilith would pop in, make a statement of fact, and then would be gone. You could not question her or see if she knew what she was talking about. As usual, they attempted to contact her but she only came at her convenience. This was probably one reason their mother had blocked her from home. She just about drove her crazy. Their mother often stated that Lilith came from the gypsy side of the family. That was not meant as a complement. Miranda had the oval face of her grandmother with skin like a shimmering pearl. Her hair was a golden wheat with streaks of yellow. This she often wore in a single braid down the middle of her back. Her eyes were the color of violet and often turned blue when speaking to the dead. John Michael had a square jaw with a mop of hair so dark it looked blue in the sun. There was a narrow strip of blond stretching from above the left ear to the back of the head almost in the shape of a snake. This was the talisman for his protective gifts. His eyes were pools of chocolate brown. Miranda was several inches taller than John Michael which he deeply resented.

The children spent the first week exploring the town. There was a malt shoppe two blocks east. This is where they ran into Butterbean. He was a sweet boy, just a little portly from his love of sweets, He was sucking up more ice cream than they had seen all year. Truth be told, he was a glutton. Eating was his religion. He lived in the parsonage of the Methodist Church. His dad was the preacher man. He was tall, lean and mean. He believed so much in the Lord that he left no room for family. His church was small as was his mind. The only ghost he believed in was the Holy Ghost. More about him later. Butterbean's mother was a jolly soul with the shape of a pear. She was short and earthy and always cooking. She even cooked for the city jail. People joked that some got arrested just to eat her cooking. She loved to laugh and was always singing. Unfortunately she had no sense of tone but everyone mentioned how nice she sang. She was truly a good person and no one tried to take that joy from her. She was much loved.

They all attended the funeral for the widow Wilson. The Baptist preacher gave a great send off which the widow appreciated. It looked as if she invited everyone who had died within the last 60 years. She was flittering about as if she was the social butterfly of death. She could not stop herself from sitting on her coffin and saying how good her corpse looked for such an old lady. Then she would just laugh and laugh which was annoying to Lilith. Yes, grandmother had come for this sendoff. She had brought her cat which kept jumping into the coffin to the dismay of the widow, She did not want to get on the wrong side of Lilith. After all, with the gifts she had in life she was almost considered spirit royalty. Miranda was having a time keeping still and respectful during the service. She had never seen spirits behave as these. It was like a party on the other side. Who would have thought of that? She did take notice that Miss Holloway had just made her entrance. She had been an old maid, she preferred bachelor woman, who had the bad luck to die three days after her mother. She looked after her for 43 years and so never had a chance to live. Therefore she was quite active in the local ghost business. Never having a chance to socialize she was doing that now. And having been a pleasant woman in life she was welcomed into the social circle of death. She had been a handsome woman but was not considered a beauty. She was the first to welcome Miranda and

Miranda was surprised to find herself liking her and enjoying her company. They would chit chat just as girlfriends will do. Her people had been here for quite some time. As a matter of fact she had been deceased so long that she had acquired some gifts through trial and error. She had a bit of power to actually move physical objects although that did make her a bit disoriented and confused. It was a different story with the girl who resided in the fire place from which she had died, This is where she could watch the families who lived there throughout the year. She did not mean too but sometimes her face was seen in the flames. That is what the children of the Sasser family saw from time to time. They were not concerned by the apparition. It was a different story the night their mother was sitting in front of the fire mending a pair of pants. The fire had died down as she thought of throwing on one last log. Looking up she saw the girl who was surprised to see the mother there. So surprised was she that she showed her burnt face. The mother screamed and awoke several neighbors who came running. She was still in her chair when they arrived, Her face was pale and her heart was racing. She screamed for such a long time they sent for the doctor. Uncle Charles arrived and gave her a sedative. As she relaxed and before passing out her story was told. The neighbors who had lived there for decades recognized the girl. Her name was Mary. She had been learning to cook when her apron caught fire. She ran into the yard where she burned to death. Families throughout the years had reported the face in the fire. Mrs. Sasser wanted to move, the children wanted to stay and the husband wanted them to just shut up. Miranda heard about this from her uncle. She called out to Mary who materialized at the home of the doctor. She was just a lonely spirit. Miranda introduced her to the Vaxley children and Stew. This arrangement worked well most of the time. There was a slight hitch. If Stew was visiting and got excited he would jump out of the fire. Mrs. Sasser had turned to a nightly toddy so that was not a big problem.

BUTTERBEAN

At the end of their first week the children walked the few blocks to the Methodist graveyard. Butterbean was going to show them the parsonage where he lived. As they turned into the church they could see the spirits walking among the graves. Miranda and John Michael always enjoyed walking through the markers of the dead. The spirits would acknowledge their presence from a distance. They were always surprised to see the living realize they were there. The twins would only respond if a spirit wanted to interact. Of course, John Michael could not speak with them so Miranda always lead the way. The dead essentially wanted to be left alone to take their path to the light. Some left right away and others still had some things unresolved which prolonged their journey. The three children were playing among the tombs when the two departed children took notice of them. It was not often that someone living could see them. But to be seen and heard was indeed a rare event. Running over to them the spirit children suddenly stopped. Butterbean was eating a pear and sprinkling it with salt which fell to the hallowed ground. The salt tied the spirits to a spot they could not overstep nor move from. They drifted into a vapor and were gone. They would have to wait for another time. Miranda had a sense that there was something different about these graves. The earth did not sound as it should if filled with graves.

Miranda's attention was suddenly turned to the white dog which was by her side. His name was Stew and considered it his job to guard the graves where he once played. His owner had been the pastor many years before. Naturally Butterbean was not aware of the abilities of his new friends. Suddenly he felt the licking of the dog on his leg. He turned the color of chalk and was frozen where he stood. Miranda laughed and called the dog to her. "Something is on my leg", he screamed as he shivered in the afternoon sun. "Oh be quiet", Miranda whispered so as not to frighten Stew. "It is just a dog who is lonely." "I do not see any dog" Butterbean screamed as he stood frozen in fear. Laughing John Michael pointed at the dog and started to explain. Calling them crazy he ran into the parsonage and slammed the door as he hollered for his father.

Old man Fletcher was the preacher man. He was one of those who took that life as a way to make a living. His faith was real but was never tested. He always knew what was right for everyone and that was essentially what he preached. He had no patience for Butterbean and ran from the rectory to see what was the matter. Butterbean was babbling about some invisible dog. Pastor Fletcher thought this was a reaction to a sugar high and told his son to shut up and be a man. There were no ghosts. And then he looked at Butterbean's face and saw signs of fear. Butterbean had never been afraid. "Dad", he whimpered, "something was on my leg and I couldn't see anything." "Come into the chapel so we can pray aside this evil," responded Pastor Fletcher. "They said it was a dog and they could see it". "Who were you with" asked his dad. "I was with Miranda and John Michael". "You mean the Boley children?" "Yes, they are my new friends" sobbed Butterbean. "I have seen that evil in their grandmother and know it to be true. You are never to play with them again as the devil will come into this house of God. They are true children of the damned."

The shadow of a darkness appeared in the stained glass window above the altar. It seemed to almost touch the forehead of the Pastor when he slumped back in his space. The ghost children had often influenced the pastor to help his congregation. He was not one to help unless it was to his advantage. If she could materialize she would help that tub of lard cross over. And there was the Locklin child, He just wanted his parents to know he was okay and with granny. He had been found one morning in his crib, dead. He had rolled over between the crib bars and the blanket. He suffocated in his sleep. Dare I mention the lady who died on her wedding night. They had such joy until she rolled of the bed and struck her head. He still sat at her grave every day. She just wanted him to move on and have a family. She was also embarrassed to be floating around in her wedding dress. Can she not get another outfit? She was sure her mother had talked him into that. My how she was going to haunt her mother for that. The list goes on and on. Let me just mention the ghost of Martha Green. In life she was a needy friend. You loaned her money, provided a roof over her head, protected her from the abusive ex, and got her a job. The first chance she gets you are stabbed in the back to her advantage. You are no longer needed. She had another one to use to advance her goals. She was the example of the old quote, "no good deed goes unpunished." She was seen as an outcast among the dead. Martha wanted to beg forgiveness for all she had hurt but lacked the humanity to understand what she had done, She was not to be forgiven, Not by those she had hurt and not by God himself. People lacking a conscience are born dead inside. She knew she was damned to hell and could no longer avoid the darkness of the collector. Miranda had been watching what remained of Martha since her arrival. She could hear her being afraid as she drifted towards the dark one. He was feeding off her despair. Soon she would be nothing but food to give him strength. With her sin it would be a feast. Lilith suddenly appeared in the chair and was petting the dog. "Children, you know dogs are not allowed in the house," and just laughed as the dog was licking her face.

"I want to warn you two again about the thin dark form with the Bower hat. Stay away from him if it appears to you. He is drawn to you for your power and will use it if he can to snare more ghost forms to take to the dark side. His form was never human but is a source which will trick you and all who follow. I call it a he but it is neither man or female. It and others like it came before man and walked the earth. It is pure evil and seems to be a large influence in the town. See Mama Lucy for protection." She smiled and left with the dog. The minions were the small beings of mischief. They went about hiding items for their own amusement, Their goal was to irritate and make people doubt themselves. Aunt Eloise knew there were a couple in her home that Lilith kept under control. She had been around them all her life and considered them almost like family. They helped her find more things than she had lost. Miranda thought them to be most interesting. She had named them This and That. When she wanted them she would call out, "This and That, where you at?" She thought this was just too funny. it did not occur to her that giving them names would give them a touch of power. Now John Michael was not a fan. They were always about the house messing with him. He was always missing his pocket knife and watch. He loved to yoyo and was always finding it somewhere in the house. He always told his twin she should not encourage them. They had no practical use. The protectors were always chasing them throughout the house. They could have caught them with ease if they had so desired. It gave them something to play with. Mama Lucy would threaten to send them on their way every time they took that damn stuffed cat. It would show up in her bed in the bath or sitting at the kitchen table. One time it was even in the stew pot. The worst time was when it was left out in the rain. The odor of wet cat hung in the air for several weeks. This was a constant source of embarrassment for the spirit of the cat. It was well known that they were vicious gossips. They would bend the truth to make it more interesting but from a germ of truth would emerge. They were the first to realize the darkness was headed to the town. They had made Lilith aware even before the twins arrived. For this she was grateful. That showed her she had been right in keeping them near. No matter what Mama Lucy and Eloise had said. She had learned ways of the dark ones from those two. That could be valuable information in the future.

Melissa Ann was the only one of the children who did not wish to move into the old Wiggins house. As they walked onto the porch she had such as sense of unease she became nauseated. Being the oldest child it was felt she was just acting out as she had loved her old room. She and her siblings moved in a few weeks before the twins arrived in town. The home of their aunt and uncle was at the other end of the block. On the third night she was in bed when the chifferobe crackedm open. Thinking nothing of this she awoke in the morning with all her clothes thrown over the bed. Calling out to her brothers to leave her alone she placed them back. Two nights later she was reading in her room when the kerosene lantern blew out. There had been no breeze through the open windows, Searching for a match she strikes and from the light of the flame she sees the form of a man. He is over ten feet and has to bend over within the room. The arms seemed to go on forever and ended on fingertips or claws. She could not even scream as she dropped the match and fainted from her fear. Awakening a short time later she leaped into bed and stayed under the covers until daybreak as she shook with fear. Running to tell her father she burst into his room and spoke of what she had seen. He told her that it was only an old house creaking and she had let her imagination get the better of her. She should be ashamed to be scared at her age. She turned and told him she knew what she saw as she left and got dressed. At breakfast one of her brothers said his bed had shaken during the night. When he awoke the bed was across the room. That night the two decided to sleep together. They took two candles and a lantern to ensure light throughout the night. Laura, a younger sister also joined them for the night. For whatever reason her room seemed cold and erie this summer night. The three settled into the bed and were soon asleep. Around three am Laura told Melissa to stop braiding her hair as it was keeping her awake. Rolling over to face Laura she saw the hair being braided by no one. The hair was up in the air but there was no one to see. No body was there. She screamed and ran again into her father's room. But this time her father believed as he witnessed the dark mass behind them in the hallway. They all fled the house for the remainder of the night and slept on the porch. After that night they took to sleeping in the front parlor. Being Baptist they called for the reverend Sloan to come and bless their home. Never having done this before he did the best he could for something he did not believe. He walked through the house holding the cross with arms outstretched as if it were a shield. He did mutter a few verses as he thought of what his wife would fix for supper. He had become a religious man as it was a good way to make a living and the church gave you a place to live. As he entered the room of Melissa he was struck with a sense of fear which quickly turned to horror. If you have little faith you cannot stand against some things of darkness. Turning around in the room he shoved aside the family and fled babbling out the front door. Lauradid say it was a good thing that door was open. No one chastened her for such a smart remark. The dark one briefly appeared on the stairway with arms outstretched. Again the family fled the house. The good reverend had fled to his church for solace. He trembled as he prayed. His faith had been challenged and he had been found wanting. He refused to return to the house. Miranda met Melissa about two weeks after their arrival. His sister and she were jumping rope on the sidewalk in front of their house. The twins were walking past and Miranda was struck by the rhyme they chanted. "When the town has turned red and the ravens are dead, only then will the town be well an no longer in danger of hell. Jump once and then jump twice. It is often the luck of the dice." She felt this to be prophecy and asked Melissa where she had learned the rhyme. It was simply something everyone knew. It was an old rhyme. Miranda joined them in jumping rope as John Michael continued on his way to the grocery. He turned and looked again at Melissa. Something was bothering him. Was something watching them in the street. He came back with rice, flour and a few odds and ends from the store. Miranda rejoined him for the walk home. Miranda was telling him he had seen a darkness around her new friend. They had both been invited to visit their new friends and their family the next day. Upon arrival the following afternoon they sat on the porch and enjoyed lemonade and tea cakes as they spoke of the town. It was a mild summer day. The birds were singing and the bees were going from flower to flower. Even with this Miranda could sense the darkness. John Michael was playing marbles with one of the brothers but kept seeing something just out of sight. As they were leaving the shadow man showed himself at the corner of the porch. They were not sure if this had ever been human as the evil was so dark. Thanking them for the day they returned home. The mother of Melissa had come to see Aunt Eloise to ask for her help. She figured the daughter of such a woman as Lilith would have the same power. Eloise told her she could be sitting on the dead and would not know. She could not help but told her about the twins and what they had done in the past. Miranda was aware of the evil twin the town. To her it seemed to have increased since their arrival. She now saw they would be putting out small fires of evil until the main event. These were exercises needed to grow their experiences. This would be needed in the future. I was agreed they would come that Friday and the children would wait outside. Reverend Fletcher overheard a member of his church speaking of the twins thinking of doing a cleansing of the Wiggins house. He was so upset he attempted to block them from the home. Melissa's father had no tolerance for the good reverend and enlisted the help of the police to send him on his way. The day was hot with no breeze as the twins stepped into the home. They walked as one up the stairs and into the bedroom of Melissa. The air was so heavy they could barely lift their legs. Their clothing hung to them and seemed to weight a 100pounds. Turning to the wall they saw the face starting to protrude as if something was entrapped. A bit of terror crossed their minds as they refocused their energy. Both walked downstairs and spoke to the family about what they had seen. They told the mother to keep everyone out of the house. She would need to leave a shovel, two fat candles, matches, a white feather and sage on the porch. They would return at sunset to begin. They walked home to eat and take a nap. At sunset they entered the home with candles lit. Both began chanting. Miranda for the entity to disperse and leave and John Michael for protection for the both of them and the family. Going room to room they remained side by side. A stiff and chilly wind began to blow the two of them apart. John Michael was blown down and out of the room. He slid out into the hall. The door slammed and Miranda was blown hard against the wall and onto the floor. As quickly as it came the wind was gone. She relit her candle which revealed the elongated figure of the black mass. She could feel the fingertips of it against her chin. Eyes had formed as it looked at her. She had never been touched by a dark entity. She was so taken aback by this touch that for a moment she was unable to focus. As the other arm touched her forehead she saw for a moment what it once was. She saw him in his yard during the closing days of the war. His entire family were swinging in the trees. He had not wanted them living in a defeated south. He was shot by the first Union soldier who passed his house. These veterans of war were taken aback by this horror. As the face was coming closer John Michael opened the door and the darkness was gone. Miranda sat on the floor to regain her composer as her twin relit his candle. He raised her up and they walked downstairs to the kitchen for some water. Setting the candles on the table they both were drained of energy. She was telling him the vision she had seen when the evil one returned. They realized what he had done had transformed him to this inhuman entity. Miranda called out to his family to help rid him from the house. She implored their return to put what was wrong to right. She called to God to take it away and throw it down to hell. She asked for justice for these deaths. The wife and children were seen coming into the parlor all dressed in white. Their radiance flooded the house. It was like a tunnel of pure light. It was the light of those who had gone to the other side. They surrounded the entity who shrilled from the pain as the horror of what he had done was realized. There was a sense of asking for a forgiveness which would never be. He disappeared in a blink as his essence was destroyed. All members of his family turned away and were drawn upwards back into the light. There was a sense of peace which filled the house. They lit the sage and used the feather to get it into all of the rooms. The place was clean. They buried the candles under the front steps to keep out the evil and make sure it could not return. Word was sent that they were done and at sunrise the family reentered the home. The twins fell into a sleep for two days. Mama Lucy was watching over them and tossed herbs from her protection ritual over them. She realized there was much to do to ensure their safety. It would be a long summer. The twins missed the fireflies that summer, They would sit in the yard to enjoy any slight breeze before going to bed. They would chit chat with the dead. Miss Holloway was often there, Melissa was now a friend and often joined them. She just might have had a crush on John Michael. He did not seem to notice that but Miranda was going to work on that.

THE PROTECTORS

The Egyptians had worshiped the feline as gods who saw the power of the shadow world in the afterlife. The cats were the hunters of the shadows. Both were entirely white and had a blue and a green eye each. This was how they could view the shadows. The only difference was one had a pink nose and the other a black. That one also had a torn ear on the right and a burn along the right back leg. Neither was given a name as that could be used to give the dark ones power over them. The family did not view them as pets They were considered sacred and were treated as such. Those two were the protectors of the family. They stayed close to home and watched the shadows in the distance. They had been caught off guard only once and that was in the house of Mama Lucy. That stain on her ceiling was a constant reminder. It had been covered with paint many times but nothing could conceal the evil it once held. The black nosed cat had been the victor and had the scars for proof. Lilith had found them in Texas at a border town which has since dried up and been abandoned. Mama Lucy had the vision of where they would be found. The mama cat was feral and had always lived off the land and avoided most people. She dug a shallow hole on top of an unmarked grave as a bed for the coming birth of her litter. She brought a recently killed field mouse and pigeon into this birthing spot. As her labor began she ate the dead things. The first four kittens were solid black and born without breath. The last two kittens were special and began to nurse. They were born with the eyes open which gave them the gift of sight for the darkness of the world. Afterwards mama cat arose and buried the dead where they lay. She sat there throughout the night on top of the grave. The break of dawn brought Lilith into the grave yard. Mama cat was about to leave when she saw Lilith. She grabbed the kittens by the neck and dropped them at her feet as she uttered a howl almost like a dog. Bending down Lilith grabbed the two and turned back to the carriage. Mother cat looked pleased and was walking away when she was scooped up by Lilith. "Not so fast my little one" she said. "You are not getting away that easily. I do not have the time to nurse your kittens. You best be coming with me." And that is how Little One joined the family. She was stuffed in later years after death. Lilith had said she just wanted her around. It was always disconcerting to see the spirit of Mama Cat with her stuffed self. There was no love lost there. Mama Lucy had caught her once trying to scratch her stuffed self. Mama Lucy knew she needed to bury that cat but could not seem to let it go.

In the far corner of Aunt Emily's back yard lived Mama Lucy who had been the wet nurse for Lilith and had served them for many years. She was 113 years of age and had the gift of second sight. She had been close to blind for many of those years and was feared by those who did not know her. She had given up cooking for the family many years before and retired to the guest house. Being much loved she was now taken care of by the aunt. Her body was frail but her mind was as sharp as a newly honed knife. True, she was as dark as night as no white blood tainted her. She was a true woman of Africa and was a dark beauty in her day. She had an African name which she kept to herself. She was well aware knowledge of her name would give power to others. Her people were the witch doctors of her tribe and were well versed in protective spirits. It was her the children sought to get some relief from the shadows. Her small parlor was warm as she always kept a fire going. She was aways cold as if a chill lived in her body. She always said, "I be cold to keep out the evil ones who are attracted to the fire and heat." She could not see the shadows but knew they were about. There was a dark stain on the ceiling in her parlor with a trace of it down one wall. This was what was left of a shadow she had cast out of her home with the help of the protectors. No one ever questioned how that was. It was just accepted as fact.

The children ran into the parlor all excited to see Mama Lucy. She called out to her babies and wrapped then in her love. She knew how special they were to be able to speak to the dead. Now if she could just teach them to view them and not get involved in their troubles. That was the only grievance she had with the white folk. Family or not, they always had to be involved. She had been visited by Lilith in her dreams and was stirring the iron pot in the fireplace. She had just placed a clump of sage onto the fire. Everyone knew this helped to remove the spirits. "What is cooking in the pot" they said as one? Being twins they often thought alike.

"A few rocks from the river to keep the spirits on the run. Some Monkey weed to keep them confused and a bit of graveyard dirt to keep them in the ground. I will capture the smoke in bottles and place a piece of iron within and top it with wax mixed with holy water. If kept on the body one will be protected", she said as she stirred it again. The odor was not too bad. Kinda like an old, wet sock drying in the sun. After a few days the odor was less.

Mama Lucy was in the rocker by the fire as she looked at the children. "There is some kind of evil lingering around the town. It is going to come after you two in order to be stronger and increase its influence. Take these bottles for protection. There are more for your aunt and uncle." They left Mama Lucy after a few hours and returned to the big house. They were content being around the family. They were happy to be a distance from their mother who was always asking so many questions about what they saw. Their answer always worried her and made her so anxious. She was never one to relax. The twins accompanied the doctor as he paid a visit to the widow Dunning. She was a shut in who lived with her two daughters and their husbands. The form was crawling up the basement stairs when John Michael was checking out the noise vibrating throughout the house. Miranda had seen a misty young man walking towards the basement who turned and gave her a look of hatred as he disappeared. The noise was growing louder. She said it had begun just a few days previously. The day her daughter remarried was the first day they had heard the sound. Miranda went to join her twin at the basement door in the kitchen. She also witnessed the form as it struggled to come up. It was such a thing of hate that the form itself was twisted and crippled. A name came to her and it was Johnny. Speaking the name she asked if that were he. It did not respond but she knew the answer. This was the first husband. He rebuked his death and was attempting to come back. It was not fair that he had died young, If he could not live again then he would take his wife to death with him. While the twins doubted he could harm the wife they realized she would want no part of this. That path of her life was over. Miranda looked hard at the form and quietly said, "silence, wail no more", and so it was. The form could not move into the house proper. He would remain at the base of the stairs until he accepted his death and moved on, There was too much hatred still in him, Like many of the living he was his own worst enemy. He only had to power to hurt himself. They walked into her bedroom where uncle Charles was checking her heart and said they had bled the water pump at the sink. The pump had become full of air and that was producing the noise. There was no need to alarm the widow. The form only they could see would keep attempting to move up with no result. And so it would always be. Wishing her a good day they left.

MISS CLAUDIA

Miss Claudia was a true example of the southern belle. Her neck was long and she had the grace and manners of a more gentle time. She was a product of the old south. Gracious and attuned to what was right and what was not. She had been dying for years in her mind. The first time she bleed at the age of 13 she knew she was dying. She just did not realize it took a lifetime of living in order to appreciate death. How sad she never really lived. She realized she was not the pretty sister but had the face of a spinster even while young. Her hair was a light brown and thin and always tied in a bun. She would tilt her head back with a general turn to the left and stare at the ceiling or the open sky to think. It was as if she fully expected the Lord to give her an answer. She was an educated lady for the time and had been seen marching for the vote. She appeared to be withdrawn and weak but like most southern girls, had a backbone of steel when provoked. She had always sensed something unnatural in the home she shared with her elderly father. She had seen things she could not explain and often felt something watching just out of her sight. Recently she had awoken with scratches like the mark of a claw across her breast. Twice she had turned over to see her doll from childhood rocking in the chair. The room was as cold as the grave. Last night she watched a shadow in her doorway who turned back and looked at her with a questionable look almost of amusement. It once had the shape of a human but was changing into a darker thing. It was hungry. It sensed her weakness. The form was dark and suddenly gone. The fear she now felt was not known to her. It was a terror and she realized she needed rescue. She arose in a cold sweat and washed her face in the bedside basin. She took a blanket and moved herself to the front veranda. There she rocked until the light of day. She was the only caregiver for her father. Captain Wiggins lived on the outskirts of town on what was a relic of his plantation home. He had left an arm on the battlefield while fighting against the federal troops. He could well recall the past but could not remember if he had had a morning meal, the day of the week or where he stayed. After feeding her dad breakfast she placed him in his rocker which she had used that night. She put a saddle on the mare and set out for town. She rode it like a man as a side saddle was a stupid thing for a rider. If she is seen well let the neighbor talk. She enjoyed the wind in her hair as she galloped down the road. She had put on the best dress she had. It might be dusty after the ride but it would have to do.

Lilith had been a friend of her mother so she was somewhat aware of the gifts of the children. As she rode into the yard Susie and the twins were planting flowers in the giant concrete urns. Miranda looked up and knew why she had come. Uncle Charles was called out of the office to help harness his carriage for his wife and children, Mrs. Wipple was leaving the office at that moment and overhead Susie speaking of the twins and the ghosts she thought that were haunting Miss Claudia. She would prove to be a gossip and soon the town would be aware of the "gifts" of the children. Some would believe but most would associate them with the devil.

It was a fairly short ride to the plantation. The twins entered the yard and saw such a large number of shadows roaming the acreage. There were slaves which were hunting the path to the other side. An angry overseer could be seen who was becoming a dark entity. A young couple were humming a sad song and walking through the cotton blooms. There was the memory of some jumping the broom, children running about and other events of an earlier time. Most were just not able to leave their life behind and would be tied to the land until they could move on. On the porch sat Miss Claudia's dad. His mind was feeble and occupied with the grandeur of an earlier day. The money was long gone and sharecroppers were working the land that had not been sold for taxes. Beside him they could see a male figure who turned their way to acknowledge them. This was the father waiting to take his son on that long journey of death. The twins wandered all about the house and saw more memories which were fading into time.

There only appeared to be two figures of evil and destruction. One was the overseer who was angry to be dead, He had been cruel in life and wanted to regain his place in controlling others and using the whip. Miranda knew he would be easy to disperse as his anger was unfocused. She walked out of the house as he would have to be displaced from the soil. He turned into a face of terror as he attempted to scare her. She told him he was not welcomed on the land as she showed him the path to hell while she sprinkled the ground with salt and a touch of holy water. His shape became longer than possible and he shrieked and was gone. There was the sighting of a lady in a hoop dress but she turned out to be but a memory replayed in time. She caused no harm and would be gone some day.

John Michael was pointing at the house to the second floor veranda across the front. The doors were open and there the ancient one resided. It was not afraid of the twins. It knew it could never be removed from the site. It had possessed the land long before the Indians populated the region. It was ancient and immortal. It simply could not be destroyed. Miranda knew it would never leave but she thought she could contain this thing of evil which loved to influence the living. Miranda entered the dusty dining room. The banquet table could seat thirty although half the chairs were broken. The velvet was faded and torn with signs of the rats that had chewed on them long ago. The pine flooring was scarred with the hoofs of the stallion the Union captain had ridden into the home and fed from the piano bench as he soiled the floor. That insult was remembered all these years later.

Miss Claudia was gathering up all the candlesticks throughout the house as Miranda requested. John Michael obtained a silver tray from the butler's pantry to catch the burning of the sage. He and Miss Claudia opened all the interior doors of the house. Miranda had just lit the first tray of sage when they heard the shouting of Pastor Fletcher. He had been visited by Mrs. Wipple who presented herself as a concerned Christian lady. Calling out to Miss Claudia he commanded her not to allow Miranda to provoke God's wrath with her heathen ways. Laughing within six inches of his face she shouted in a voice which was no longer sweet nor pure, "Little man, you are too ignorant to realize there are strange and evil things which predate religion. You knew Lilith and her powers yet you called her evil for the things you are too rigid to understand. I sought help that you could not give me."

A little over two years ago she had reached out to Pastor Fletcher. He did not believe in the things she said she saw but agreed to bless her house. He came and walked from room to room making the sign of the cross and reading random passages from the old testament. He would occasionally call for any unclean entities to depart. When he started to observe his breath he realized the room was ice cold. Startled and confused he looked up from the good book as there was the face of a clown with nothing but a twisted mouth with teeth descending from the chandelier. Each crystal held a different face of horror. He lost bladder control and peed all over the floor. He could not utter a sound and was too terrified to move. It was only a moment but he felt as if he had been staring at the thing for a very long time. He suddenly felt his legs again as he backed out of the room. He fled without so much as a goodbye.

Miss Claudia found his cross on the floor that evening. When he next saw her in church she attempted to return his cross. "Keep it", he said, "I am sure it is not mine." He made no mention of his encounte r as accepting what he saw was not in his world view. He had to protect his sanity and belie f system. Some people do not chose to learn. "If you are such a man of God", she shouted, "then come inside the house to show me there is nothing here." He turned and left whipping his horse down the road with Miss Claudia hurling insults at his back. She had no patience for stupid. She could see the fear in him and realized what a weak man of faith he was. John Michael was standing in the doorway of the dining room after having said a prayer of release in each of the rooms. He left burning sage on each hearth. Miranda nodded and lit the candles and sage as they exited the house. The rooms quickly filled with the smoke of the sage. From the veranda could be seen the image of the dark one in the coffin doors which were the entrance to the house. Walking around the home they laid a double ring of salt and left an opening in front of the coffin doors which were the formal entrance into the home. Walking in different directions each laid a circle of salt. This double ring was left with a gap in front of the doors. Holy water was sprinkled onto the threshold as they said the incantation to tie the evil to the earth. Suddenly they opened the doors and shouted for the shadow to leave. In but a moment it was outside the house. They immediately closed the circles of salt. They heard the silent scream of the entity as it took notice that it had been displaced. It was weaker at this point and slowly dispe rsed into the earth. Wagon loads of salt were thrown around the foundation which kept the ground barren and safe. The plantation had a history of death and cruelty. It was now just an old southern mansion slowing going to ruin. As they rode back to town Miss Claudia was watching them while putting down her hair. It was time for her to live. She turned to bring the general in and realized he had passed. His one arm was pointing where the evil had gone. There was a faint smile on his face. Miss Claudia sat by him and placed the arm down by his side. His war was now over.

The funeral of Captain Wiggins was all about the war. His valor and belief in the south was discussed as was his loss of an arm on the field of battle. What a hero he had been to his men. How great he looked atop that horse. His ghost was listening to the burial and thinking what a bunch of crap. He had been scared as hell in every battle. His arm had been loss during a fight while he was drunk and waving an ax. He was no hero. Just a lucky man to return home. He now realized wars are never won and most doers of bravery are liars. He was pleased the house had been cleaned of the evil and his daughter would be safe. He was happy to finally be freed from the crimes of the south.

TENT REVIVAL

The tent revival was advertised as "Five Days with the Lord" throughout the community. It was always held in the heat of summer as if that alone would show the fires of hell. The huge white tent was erected in the park by the river. The good citizens would be bringing food to share during the evening services. The hard benches were being setup on Monday morning. Sawdust had been placed on the ground to absorb the dampness of the river bottom. That first night was overseen by the Methodist minister, Butterbean's dad. He preached a rather dull sermon on morality with the young people paying him no mind. He was never one who enjoyed expanding his ministry. He had the congregation of his church and thought that was enough to manage. Butterbean was eating some food his mother had prepared and was trying hard to look down the breast of Pearl, a young girl of beauty. He only had to go on the Methodist night and saw the twins from a distance. He did walk over after a while and asked how they were. He kept a fair distance. He did not know what other tricks they might play.

Night two was better received as the Baptist had brought their featured singer who had the voice of the angels. No one recalled his sermon but it was short so most approved. A few empty bottles of whiskey were found after he spoke and some were cautioned not to bring drink again. This was a time to speak of faith and not party. The reverend Sloan reminded them of why they were there.

A preacher from a community over the hills was coming as a guest speaker on night three. The weather had turned to showers which just added to the humidity of the night. There was a tint of green in the sky as the thunderstorms passed. An odd chill seemed to linger in the hot summer night. The twins were going to attend as they had a sense of the evil about to come. The dark figures about the house were clinging to the roof while attempting to enter. The sage, salt and holy water were keeping them out.

Aunt Eloise and Uncle Charles were seated on the third row back. The twins entered the tent and sat in the last row left. This would give them a view and some protection from the evil influence. Naturally they had the bottles of protection Mama Lucy had prepared. They were the only two who would recall the events of that night. Miranda was about to call Aunt Susie and Uncle Charles to join them in the back. She had had a brief vision of death to come. And for whatever reason, she felt like there was a hollow sound in the ground. Something was very wrong. But then a tall, dark figure strutted into the tent once the benches were crowded with the faithful.

It was quite easy to see that he was well fed and well dressed. Miranda wondered how he moved all that bulk around. The figure reminded her of the muscle men at the circus. He did not possess the muscle but had all of their bulk. He turned immediately and looked at the children with a smirkon the face and a twinkle in his eye. He even tipped his hat. John Michael whispered the incantation for protection in the nick of time, you could see the anger on the face of "the man". His goals would not be fulfilled this night. Afterwards the audience could only recall that he was a dark figure. Some said he wore an overcoat of black. He was also described as having a silver buckle about the waist and rings of gold on each finger. Widow Grimes remembered the smell of sulfur which reminded her of a grave. Some recalled the blackness of his eyes but there was not much more they could remember. Now who did he remind her off? She was 96 and had to ponder that memory for a while. Mrs. Basque was the first to recognize the evil. After all, she was so big in the church. She was always letting her Sunday school class know the gossip about others. She figured she was the most holy as she was such a great judge of everyone else. As he began to speak in a voice which was hypnotizing the audience she called out to God as she raised her hands to heaven, If she had been a true believer she could not have been struck down so easily. She was surrounded in a rush by several dark shadows and died with a look of horror etched upon her face. The children could sense the ones in attendance who thought she got what she deserved. Mr. Katz, an older Jewish man from the old country who had once studied the Torah, stood up in his seat and called upon the old gods of the sabbath for the extermination of this evil. He had seen this in the forests of Germany among the peasants. He lingered a bit longer but also died stricken with the terror the dark had brought. Alonzo Cain called out for the gathering to pray for deliverance from this darkness. This evoked such a laugh of evil that Alonzo and several others simple dropped into death as if that was a refuge. And then the preaching began. The children were transfixed and each clasped the metals hanging from their necks.

They could honestly not recall his sermon from hell. It was concerning chaos and how there is no rhythm of the universe. But the children saw the rhythm. It was at this time that they recognized it had something to do with the town's history, They had never seen such horror and hoped to not see it again. All they knew was that something had come back. The evil had not been dispersed in the past and that was why Sugar Lot kept attracting evil. There was more than just sugarcane surrounding the town. The shadow knew how to put on a show as a choir of 8 approached the stage. They seemed to glide down the aisle as there was no jumpy rhythm of walking. It was around then that a scream arose. This was a choir of the dead as their feet never touched the ground. Several fainted when the kerosene light was seen through them. It was thought some pretended to faint in order to see and not be seen. Terror hung in the air like a curtain, Seated on the front row was Mr Barnett, the owner of the bank and a leading citizen, It was obvious he did not know when to leave well enough alone. He was a deacon of his church and liked to have the town follow his lead. He knew best what his neighbors needed as he was just so educated. It was about this time that Mr. Barnett, a portly man who loved his food and drink, called out and demanded to know just what was going on? Pointing his claw finger at Mr. Barnett his mouth began to fill with coins. Two members of the choir approached as coins fell from their mouths into his. He tried to stand but collapsed. This lasted but a minute..

The following morn he was found with a pocket of change about his feet. His head was on his shoulders facing his back. When entering the tent the chief of police just stood in horror of the scene. He could hear those behind him begin to vomit. Each corpse was seated with the hands bound as if in prayer. The wooden cross on the stage was upside down. A hint of rotten eggs remained along with other scents. As the town awoke seven dead were found within the tent. At the entrance was the body of a man no one knew. He had a cross of copper and a star of David. Each of which had left a burn on his arms. The cross had burnt so deep the right arm was close to detaching. The only clue was the red and black tattoo behind his right shoulder, There was a hastily drawn triangle in the dirt at his feet. It could easily be seen as being broken because a copper fork had transversed the equilateral triangle. The sides were no longer equal.

The police had been called when the bank failed to open at 10:00 am. The husband of Mrs. Wipple was hunting for her as were several others who awoke to find the family members who had not come home the night before. The odor of the dead was drifting down the street as the sun warmed up the morning. It was akin to the smell of sulphur and iron ore. The animals caught a whiff and walked away, snarling. There would not be a revivalthe next night. The people of the town stayed home, read their Bibles and gossiped about their fears and whom to blame.

Naturally they thought of the twins. All this trouble started when they came. They knew what had been done at the home of Miss Claudia. They knew what Mrs. Wipple had said before her demise. They all had known about the powers of Lilith. Pastor Fletcher had just preached a good sermon about the evil children in their midst. Yes, he probably overstated but never the less, everything was believed. The town had begun to avoid the children and their aunt and uncle. His practice had suffered as the ladies were reluctant to enter the home of children who they felt to be abnormal and an insult to God. They were waiting for God to strike them dead in Church but that never occurred. The baptist pastor was leary of them but did not turn them from the church. All of this saddened aunt Susie as many friends had turned against them. Her only pleasant thought was that at least now she knew her true friends. Being that her husband was the only doctor she knew they would be back. She would see to it that there were no more friend discounts. They removed the dead and then left that place of horror alone. They would need a while to investigate the deaths. The police chief was sure they had a murder in their mist, He did not equate this with any supernatural force. The children knew something was coming and started to prepare.

THE GRAVEYARD

The graveyard continued to draw the twins. They could sense the spirits of the children had something to say. Perhaps it was why they had not gone to the light. Were they aware of what was happening in the town? They had not seen Butterbean since the night of the revival. Pastor Fletcher had spoken harshly to Uncle Charles about the twins bringing in evil. He viewed them as unclean beings who awoke the dead. They did not belong is his world. They were a danger to his narrow belief system. Not unlike that Darwin fella who was attempting to destroy God. Uncle Charles told him the evil was already there and a huge argument ensued resulting in a bloodied nose and a black eye for the pastor. Needless to say they did not go to his church that coming Sunday. This was especially bad as Charles was a deacon of the church and his absence was well noted. That was the Sunday the pastor called out the evil he saw in the twins. Their summer was no longer carefree. Naturally the pastor told his son to keep away. The ghost children were sitting on a bench almost in the center of the graveyard when the twins arrived. Behind them was one of the larger markers which displayed their names with a date of death as 1848. The girl had been called Savannah and Jackson was her brother. They were the Vaxley children who had lived in the house of aunt Eloise. It had been built by their father as a family home. They had died of Typhoid Fever after lingering for about a week. They were holding hands as they passed. They held no malice and seemed pleased to see the twins again. Stew had come back with them and jumped onto the bench. You could not see his hind legs when in such a happy mood. Savannah was the first to speak. Miranda could sense a level of desp air in the tone of her voice. Looking towards the parsonage and the ghost path in the back she began to speak of her fear of that path. It was always calling them forward. They could see the spirits and "those other things". Some shadows would wander off the path as they were drawn to the aurora of the living. The saving grace was the fact that those vile creatures could not walk on the hallowed ground. Miranda had noticed an echo in the ground the first time walking there. Like hollow ground. It was no longer hallowed. The vaults echoed with the caskets beneath their feet. Soon the darkness will encompass the graves and the occupants will be lost to eternity. So they had sought out the twins for help. John Michael had a look on his face he had when eating sour balls. The only difference is his tongue was not red and yet he had a look of disgust. "You cannot think that we have any control over things such as are moving along that path. You two are crazy ghosts." Miranda just smiled and said, "We need to go. If something can be done we will have to try."

"Thank you said the sister" as she stuck out her tongue at John Michael. Again, he was surprised. What type of ghosts are these he thought? They forget their place. He was just a bit prideful. He was a young boy after all. They turned to the sidewalk and that was when Butterbean was seen watching from the steps of the church. He just looked and finally waved weakly at the two. He wanted to approach then but his dad was near and would have made a scene. The stained glass that the shadow had arisen from had a large crack making a triangle of equal sides. This piece of glass had turned a muddy black. The afternoon sun cast a shadow from the glass that fell upon the feet of the Blessed Virgin who was the mother of Mary. As the sun set the image was clothed in the shadow. He was afraid. The ghost children shuttered as if a cold wind had come. Being ghosts they had not been cold since death. There seemed to be a doorway with lines of the dead and other dark things going along the path in back of the Methodist Church. It went into the woods for a good distance. Over the years several people happened upon this path which could not be seen by the living. They did not return. Well, that is a lie. That young girl who walks the square every day was rumored to have walked down that path. She had gone to place flowers on the grave of her mother about three years past. When she did not return home for dinner the town formed a search party. They searched high and low for five days. Her father searched even longer to no avail. The search dogs lost the scent in back of the graves and howled. The dogs could not be persuaded to go into the woods. They could sense the terror there. Six months later she suddenly appeared in the graveyard from which she had disappeared. Her dress was the same and had no sign of dirt and disarray. She had a mark like a claw running across her right shoulder. It had healed. Her hair was now streaked with gray and her eyes were wild. She was found without speech. She had lost the ability to form a constructive thought. Since her return she would walk until dark at which time her father would bring her in. It was rumored she would become wild when walking by the church. While walking back home the twins were again passing the statue on the square. The ghost of the man was trying to get the pigeons off his statue to no avail. The twins walked over and shooed away the birds. The shadow of the man did not say a work but looked at them in appreciation. They nodded and moved on. This was when they paused and said hello to Miss Jeanette. Now she confused the twins. They were there when Preacher Fletcher was giving the sermon on death and passing over to Jesus. He was taking questions from the congregation when she asked how someone overcame the fear of dying, Looking directly at her he asked, "Are you not a Christian?"

"Of course I am" she said.

"Do you accept Jesus as the Christ?"

"Of course I do", she stated.

"Well then, why do you fear death? You either believe or you do not."

All could see the fear on her face and her crisis of faith. She was a lip service Christian. That was how she was raised. She had always just accepted this religion and never thought of how or why. She was the example of most Christians who followed Christ as that was the norm. Their faith had no substance. Had they been born a Jew, they would be waiting for the true Messiah. If born a Muslin they would be praying to Allah. Perhaps this was why the evil was present in the town. There were few true believers like Butterbean's mother. She lived her faith and hoped others would do the same. If all were such as she the evil would have no hold on the town.

Seeing the moment of your death is either a relief or a fearful thing. For Nancy Hellstone it was a blessing as she had been sick all those years. She welcomed her end and expected to be in the presence of the Lord. That is why when her spirit arose in front of her sister at the grave she was none too pleased. It was well known sister was not a good Christian. So ever since her death she had been seeking the light. The way of the Lord. The right hand of God. There had obviously been a record keeping error. Just like in life she had to take care of everything herself. It was yet to occur to her that she might be seeking something that was not available to her. If truth be told she was on the same level as that Martha Green. She too had used people during her life. Some are just born with darkness of the soul as were these two.

She was always in church but that was just a pose. She had no social skills. She was like an actor in a play. She knew the lines but had no sense of their meaning. The darkness would swallow her ghost soon enough. She had no redeeming attributes. For her life she was viewed as she appeared to be. Few knew who she really was.

The good reverend had been laying on the grave alone with his dreams of the darkness. He had felt compelled to walk the graves since the twins arrived. He finally arose and placed a handful of soil in his pocket. Communion was tomorrow. The congregation would drink the wine and eat the bread of the Christ. His sweet wife always mixed and baked the communion bread representing the body of Christ. Of course she was not aware that he had placed graveyard dirt into the flour. She had commented last Sunday morn about the dirty look and bitter taste but there was no time to bake again. And now for the second week it again was not up to her standard. Reverend Fletcher had no knowledge of what he had done. Having walked down that path of darkness which extended into the woods he was no longer a man of faith, he was just a vessel for the darkness to come. That Sunday the congregation tore into the communion bread as if it was the last meal to be had. They had never consumed a loaf with such flavor. It was the flavor of evil, about like dark chocolate. The flavor of all anyone could want. They had no memory of this. After church many more had signs of the rash as they wandered down the paths by the graveyard. They saw things which were never meant to be seen. This ground had been tainted. This was the way the demon would return and had returned in the past. The Vaxley twins were watching this in increasing fear for the twins, themselves and the town. They could see the signs of the return of the evil.

Go to church or the devil will get you. That was the sign Everlasting Marble wore around town most days. He was named Everlasting cause his mama had thought her birthing of him would never end. Truth be told it took over five days because she just did not want to push. He did have the gift of second sight but could not process the information, His mama had dropped him on his head a few times and if this played a part was just not known. Anyway, he had been in trouble as a kid and spent a few years in prison. Oh yes, he had found the Lord in his cell. Like one possessed he clung to this to give his life meaning. He lived with his sister and her family as he had never held down a job for any length of time. So each morning he entered the square and began the day frightening people to go to church. The spirit of the soldier on the square had enough of these tactics. So one morning he showed himself to this preaching man. He thought this would jar him back to reality. He was so wrong. Everlasting saw him as an angel from the Lord. That was when he was sure he was doing the right thing. He was still peaching the day a carriage ran over him in the road. He assumed the Lord would protect him, him being a believer and all that. He died instantly and sat on the roadside taking it all in. That was when he realized there was a difference between those of true faith who used faith as a way to shield their life from others. He no longer had the need to seek faith. He now knew what he had always needed to know, The spirit of the soldier did not understand. But then again each spirit has a different path to the Almighty as they deem him to be.

ANGRY MAN

The young couple next door had been given the home of the husband's grandfather after his death. They had been reluctant to accept this gift as the grandfather had been an angry man. He never bonded with his children and had no time for family. He was always reluctant to have anyone in his home. The grandson did not think he could be comfortable living there. But it was a nice home in a good neighborhood and his wife was insistent. They had been living there for a couple of years and had two young daughters. They started to upgrade the home to the modern standard. This is when the trouble began.

Tools went missing, the labors heard voices telling them to leave and some reported being slapped. Many refused to return. They did not believe the workmen until the night something kicked the puppy across the kitchen floor. Sarah, the wife, had been home alone and ran screaming into the night. She was still in her apron and could not be calmed. Aunt Eloise heard Sarah and rushed outside with the twins. Miranda could see the grandfather in the yard shaking his fists and shouting at her to leave his house alone. Looking his way she shouted. "For God's sake shut up." Turning he saw her and hurried back inside. No one had ever seen him before and this had given him a bit of a shock. The following morning Aunt Eloise walked next door to see what she could do. She found the couple speaking of moving but they could not decide what to do. They just did not have the money. There had always been a touch of uneasiness within the house. This was attributed to the wind, noises from the street or the old house settling. The few times they saw a shadow was easily blamed on the gas lighting throughout the house. The oldest child was but three and had spoken of the man on the landing several times. They now realized that a spirit was in their home and no longer felt the children were safe. Sarah was telling them she had been rolling the dough for biscuits when the room turned ice cold. Looking up she saw the puppy growling at nothing. She was smiling at him for barking at nothing when he let out a yelp and flew across the room into the broom closet. Something large crossed across the room and was gone. They had no clue as to what was going on. It was at this time Eloise told them what Miranda had seen down the street. She described the man with a handlebar mustache who was full of anger. Immediately the grandson realized it was his grandfather. He had not believed in ghosts but was now a believer. They spoke of what to do and hoped Miranda and John Michael could help.

Come Friday evening the twins approached the house. Their aunt and uncle stayed on their porch with the young family. Miranda was keeping the spirit focused on the two of them. She did not see this spirit as evil. He was just stubborn. John Michael walked about the house muttering his spells of protection. He did not have any sense of danger but could hardly think as the spirit kept yelling at him to get out. Miranda saw the spirit immediately. He was not afraid of them. "Get out of my house. I live here not you," he roared in a most powerful voice. Miranda was taken aback at such a strong resistance. She had never seen a mere ghost with such a strong resolve. After lighting the incense on the parlor table she engaged the spirit in conversation. This while John Michael was going room to room to leave smoke from the sage. "You do not live here" Miranda shouted. "You died in this very house several years ago. It is past time for you to cross over and follow your wife. Go towards the light." "Bull shit. I have no wish to join the wife and you do not need to shout, I am dead, not deaf. She was a nagging cow who never made anyone happy." Miranda flushed at hearing such language and fell silent. John Michael entered the room as he repeated the mantra for the spirit to leave. Turning his way the spirit broke out into a joyful laughter. "Jesus Christ. I am not going anywhere. Give it up tund tell them to put my house back together." Despite herself Miranda found herself liking this rascal. Obviously, he was too set in his ways to be forced out of the house. He had no inclination nor will to go. She entered the kitchen and poured a cup of coffee. Aunt Eloise would say she was too young for something so strong. She sat at the table as John Michael followed into the room. He spotted the biscuits and found some jam. The spirit was leaning against the sink and playing with the water. He figured that unless the girl had magic the house was his. He had not had this much fun in years. Yes, he liked these children. They were not afraid. After sipping the coffee and telling John Michael not to be a glutton, she smiled at the spirit. "Why don't we compromise?" "Why would I agree with that? You cannot evict me unless I agree to leave." "True words you speak. You can stay while the house is redone and you are no longer at ease here. What will that gain you?" He pondered that thought. "Since you are too stubborn to leave perhaps you can coexist with your family. You agree not to disturb them and they will agree to respect your space and not touch a room of your choice." Hearing this, John Michael did not think that would work. You cannot reason with a spirit. Who had ever heard of that? The spirit said, "Merciful Jesus, do you have to light that stinking mess again? You would think folk would leave me alone as I am dead. Alright, I agree. Have them put my chair back in my office where I died. Oh, and tell those girls no yelling in the middle of the night. I need the quiet." And so it was. During this time Uncle Charles began to inquire of his patients what they knew of the history of the town, No one seemed to know anything until Mr. Manchester came in for his gout. After the lecture about what not to eat Uncle Charles asked the question. Looking towards the door and pausing for quite some time he spoke. "The only thing I know concerns the Methodist graves. As you well know I lost my wife a good while back. I often would go to visit the grave. I began to take note of the tombstones surrounding our plot. The Cain markers are not together. The husband, Max, had a grave marker in front. Way in the back, on the right side, is the markers of Evelyn, his wife. There is the Taylor family with five kids. Not a one are together. Now why would you bury your children all over the grave yard?" Most of the earlier markers appear displaced. I told Arthur, a fishing friend of mine, that I believed some graves had been moved and the ground was empty. I figured they had only moved the markers. Well, a good while back we were drinking. That was when I drank before the gout got so bad. Anyway we decided to go dig up a grave to see if it was empty. So we were there choosing the grave to dig. I told Arthur to quit patting me on the shoulder. It was only when I looked up and saw him standing opposite of me that I got scared. Next thing I knew I was almost home and the alcohol was out of my system. A minute later Arthur passed me. We never spoke of this and did not return for the shovels. That was my last visit to the grave of my wife and the last time I drank. There is some kind of darkness in Sugar Lot. Even the air seems heavy. I stay home after dark as do most of my neighbors. I go to the Baptist Church now. I will only see the

Methodist Church again when they bury me there by the wife, The mirror that hung in the entrance was painted over in the home of Mrs. Mellon. The frame was very ornate and held a wide bevel. How strange it had been painted all in white. Mrs. Mellon said the house was haunted by her daughter Violet. The daughter had been engaged to a Yankee from Boston. Mrs. Mellon was not about to allow a northern dog be the father of her grandchildren. She sent him on an errand downtown to the very street where the thimble ladies walked. Having already paid for the seduction she waited with eager anticipation. He returned to the home not realizing he had been set up. Violet smelled the cheap perfume which lay over him like a sheet. She saw the blond hairs on his shirt. The look of disgust shown on his face told her all she needed to know. Not even seeking a denial she rain out the door and straight to the bridge. She leaped into the water as the current took her downstream. Her last thoughts were of hatred for her mother. She could see her hand in this. They used grappling hooks in order to retrieve the body three days later. She had gone quite a distance as her life and body floated away. The corpse was set out in the second parlor. Due to the days in the water the coffin was closed. As the quests left the home they had to pass through the entrance where a grand mirrorhung. To a person each one gasped for standing in the mirror was the daughter. The image was soaked. The dress was wet. Her dead eyes followed everyone walking beneath the mirror. The figure was again present the next day and the day after that. Mrs. Mellon figured this could be controlled by painting the mirror. True, the figure was now covered but any time Mrs. Mellon entered the home she was met by a wailing sound which was constant. It never ended and never paused. Violet intended to keep her mother out of the house. The twins were sent for and Mrs. Mellon begged for their help. As soon as she entered the house she sensed what the mother had done. She saw there was no remorse and did not intend to cast out the spirit. She and John Michael could see the paint was cracked and peeling off the mirror. The twins were able to scrap off a large portion of the paint. And there stood Violet in the full glory of her death. Mrs. Mellon was just walking through the door as Violet was walking out of the mirror. Seeing her deceased daughter so unexpectedly gave her pause. It took a few moments for her heart to stop as she gazed on Violet. The shock had been too much. Uncle Charles pronounced her dead and commented on her face. It was a study in horror. Violet simply stepped over her mother and entered the light of death. Mrs. Mellon was not missed.

FOUNDER

All that the family knew was that a doctor had founded the town and he was rumored to be a spiritualist. He was a wealthy man for that time who made a fortune with the east Indian Tea trade. He came into the area in the late 1700's when it was a small trading post at a cross roads. It was near the river for shipping, had great forests for wood and the land was for sale. After purchase of a large amount of acreage he found a graveyard to be in the center of his holdings. He built a sawmill and planned the sites for the churches he envisioned and businesses of trade. He brought in his family of eight and built the town. And that is about all anyone knew. Most did not even know his name. Several folk did say he had been run out of New York. Some said for a murder and others said for an affair with another man's wife which begat a child. It was probably for something more sinister but that would never be known.

Aunt Eloise was also hot on the trail of discovery. She was hunting the living kin of the founder. She had been surprised to realize no one seemed to have heard his name. She began at the Baptist church as she thought he might be buried there. This was a rather plain building with an impressive entrance of 66 steps to the double doors of copper. The two oaks on either side were ancient. There was a design pounded onto the doors of the river Styx and the dead being ferried to the other side. What a disturbing thing to have at the entrance to a Christian church. Walking among the graves she discovered nothing. She spoke with the pastor who knew nothing. He seemed to be on edge as he hurried her out of the church. He was just a bit hesitant to speak with Eloise due to the twins and rumors he had heard. She next walked over to the Catholic Church. It also had a grand entrance of 66 steps. The front door was carved marble of religious scenes. There were two immense figures of Saints on either side of the entrance. To her relief the priest was an educated man of faith who allowe d her to see the history of the church. She was very interested to learn the three early churches had been activated at the same time early in the history of the town. This priest knew a little about the founder and was quite verbose in the telling, About the only things known about the man was centered around his death. He had a large estate for that time. The family consisted of himself, his wife and 8 children and their spouses. There were 48 grandchildren from toddler to young adult. The family is thought to have been dead for 5 days to a week. They were discovered when a farmer passing by thought it odd there did not seem to be anyone about. He also heard the horses in the barn kicking their stalls. This was only done in times of hunger or fear. He walked to the front door and called out to anyone who might be there. That is when he noticed the odor of death and the smell of sulphur. He began to be afraid and rode back to the village for help. When the villagers arrived they had to break down the door to the room which held the corpses. It had been locked from inside. The heavy key had remained in the lock. Upon opening the door a wind rushed out of the room. The inside of the doors were charred and much of the glass had been melted in the windows, The room itself was odd if for nothing more than the heavy black drapery over the immense windows. The paint on the walls was of such a deep blood red that it looked black. There was a rolled up rug at the back of the room. Drawn in red on the wooden floors was a hugh triangle with equal sides. The four elements were drawn in the triangle. They were fire, air, water and earth as represented in symbols. Sitting on the fire symbol was Dr. Lynch, the founder of the town. Only his head and shoulders were visible. His melted torso was displayed in a hardened puddle. The look of horrorfrozen on his face was never forgotten by any who viewed the room, His children covered the lines of the triangle. Their heads had been placed with care to mimic the symbol for sulphur. That would have been an equal sided triangle sitting on a cross. The grand kids were still holding hands behind their parents. Perhaps I should not say holding as they were actually fused together. It was as if the hands had melted like wax and hardened again. They had to saw these children apart in order to collect the corpses for the grave. They could not find the wife until later that day. Someone sawing the children had to look away from his actions for a moment. That is when he saw the legs hanging from the ceiling. Some force must have thrown her like a rocket to the moon. They had to go to the roof to extract her. The head was still attached but held the shape of a plate. The local men of God came to bless the family and said a prayer for each family member. Afterwards the good reverend Vanderson retired to the Methodist church and hung himself in back of the altar. His Bible was on the podium with words he had written across the first page of Geneses. Things that never were to be are. Even God can not keep them contained. Pray. Aunt Eloise had to sit down and gather her thoughts after hearing of this horror. The priest brought her a cup of coffee with a strong dash of bourbon to steady her nerves. She was now afraid for the twins and for what they knew. Knowledge could be a danger in the hands of some.

He then continued, "The townspeople were quite concerned about this evil they had seen. Some called for the bodies to be burnt with the house and then blessing the site. It was not known if an individual or the town set fire to the house. It is recorded that the town had the smell of sulphur for quite some time afterwards. It is not known if the site was blessed nor even where it was in relation to the town. His name was not spoken again and only the dates of death are on the tombstone. The townspeople were ever fearful and no mention was made again about the event. Do you wish to see the tomb?" Looking a bit rested she followed the priest outside. The sun was high in the cloudless sky. There was the tombstone in the shape of a cross with the date of death repeated sixty six times. She now understood they were buried in a mass grave. There were no names on the marker. She thanked the priest and was about to turn away when she asked the question she feared. "being a man of God what do you think really happened that night?" You could tell from his facial expression he was thinking how to phrase his reply and if he should just lie. He knew some did not really want to hear the truth. She had said she had a need to know. Looking directly into her eyes he asked if she wanted his true telling about the subject. With a deep breath she replied, "yes, I need to know for the sake of my family." "I believe he summoned a messenger from hell that he failed to control. You know we Catholics believe in hell." He then winked at her and returned to the church. She noticed him crossing himself as he passed the grave. She had recognized the salt all over the grave. Someone was making sure the good doctor stayed dead. She went home to inform the others. Miranda was excited about this news. She called out to the Lynch family to find what had occurred when they died. All she had needed was a name to connect with them. This was a request and not a summoning. A summoning was a command. Miranda did not possess that type of power. She was unable to sense any members of their family. This had never occurred to her so she searched again with the same result. She ony saw the swirling mass of the void which she was unable to follow. She found it difficult to believe that there were no memories of their existence, She called out to Lilith with no response. What type of evil had it taken to destroy the very substance of their family? Miranda began to have doubts about confronting this evil. They would have to draw heavily on their lineage. St. Margaret the Queen of Scotland and her third son, King David, also known as St. David. Miranda wore the medal of she and John Michael, of he. John Michael saw the box. It was nothing but an old metal spice safe sticking out of the ground. He could just make out the engraved L written in a fancy script across the lid. Those were popular when spices were expensive and kept under lock and key. He had been drawn to the park by the river. He noticed a big fella there that was pacing back and forth. He seemed happy and content. This was about the time he noticed something in his mind. Almost as if the box was calling out to him as he turned about. And there it was. John Michael dug it out of that Alabama clay which soon covered him. He would have to sneak in so Aunt Eloise would not see him. He could well imagine the third degree she would give him. Running into the house he called out to Miranda about the box. His aunt had just entered the parlor and screamed at him to go outside and remove those filthy clothes, She could already see the red tracks from his shoes. Miranda had heard from Mama Lucy where they had been speaking about the protection loaf. It had to be cute with a copper knife in a specific way. Miranda walked into the back yard where John Michael was sitting on the swept ground, He was using a buther knife which was much too big to pry open the box. My he is so dirty she thought. Why can't boys never stay clean? She knew she would never marry. Inside were six identical tins with lids. It had not held spice for a very long time. Two were nothing more than rust. One was half empty with dirt. Sniffing it he recognized graveyard dirt. The next tin was almost flattened and the contents, if any, could not be determined. The last two were heavily dented but could be opened. One had three mummified fingers with one wearing a bloodstone ring. This was an older stone of healing thought to be a substance of hell. It burns a blood red and gives off a blue light. His excitement at this discovery was waning as he felt the whole think reeked of evil. A shiver ran over his body and jumped to Miranda. A sudden fear was in the air as he slammed down the lid. He was not aware until later that he had pinched his palm. The twins were frozen for a moment within this sphere of fear and then it was gone. They had met fear before and knew how to kick it away. They could not afford to hold fear but had to know how to release it in a helpful way. Fear could always be a symbol of power when used to one's advantage. That evening after John Michael had a good bath and they were in the parlor after the evening meal, Uncle Charles spoke up. "I have read in the paper that a balloonist will be in town for the next few days. If he does not over charge what say we go to the park tomorrow and see. Children, would you be afraid to ride?" Naturally they could not wait to ride. Aunt Eloise looked at her husband and you could tell she was not sure if this was a good thing to do. What if something went wrong and they were hurt. Her sister would never forgive her. Are not balloons dangerous to ride? She was just about to open her mouth when Miranda and John Michael both knew what she was about to say. "Oh" said Miranda with a startle in her voice. "Are you okay Miranda," asked Aunt Eloise with a look of concern. "I apologize" Miranda responded. "I just had a visit from Lilith. She showed me a vision of our balloon ride". She grinned with ease.

The balloon man was set up at the green space by the river. Many were leary of going up but a line was already forming. He was assured of a good day. The twins were there watching his crew blowing up the balloon with hot air. Butterbean had already taken a place in line. He waved them over so they joined him in the line. He seemed to be less afraid of them. His mother had taken him aside and explained there was nothing wrong with those twins, People always feared what they did not know, She said his father was wrong but he was a good man. She did not want him to be of a narrow mind. Butterbean was glad to see them and spoke of his dad passing out in the church and calling a name. He said it was Nybbas. Miranda made a mental note to visit that church. The line was moving forward when their aunt and uncle ran up. They had been delayed due to a carriage horse crashing into a store front. They had been walking to meet them and Mr.

Barkley had just passed in his carriage. Without any warning he called out a name they did not recognize and the horse galloped into the place glass window. The horse only had a few cuts but Mr Barkley was dead. Uncle Charles ran up to help and and found the corpse covered with the same rash he had seen on four other members of the Methodist church. He could not determine a cause of death. Something was very wrong. He could smell the fear coming off the corpse. He was afraid. Counting the operator there was room for six in the woven basket which held the balloon. Aunt Eloise noticed it first as the balloon ascended and she had started to relax. The park was a perfect triangle. Viewed from her perch it was a perfect equal sided triangle. The ancient oaks on the left, limestone on the right with the river at the bottom made it impossible to see from the ground. Miranda also saw the triangle but noticed another thing. There appeared to be depressions all about the ground. This was slight as if something had been removed and over time the ground settled. If it had not been for the afternoon sun casting shadows this would not have been see n. Quickly she realized this must be the site of the graveyard that had been removed all those years ago. It appeared that not all graves were gone. Now she understood what had helped power the dark one at the revival. It had taken place on ground which had once be hallowed and was now defiled. Miranda now knew a little better what needed to be done. They just might have a chance after all. She just wanted a little more information.

Butterbean was looking at his dad's church when he saw the oddest thing. If the roof lines of the three churches were joined they would form a triangle. He pointed this out to Miranda who had the strangest look on her face. He asked John Michael if he saw it to, but he was airsick and had just realized he was afraid of heights. He was too occupied with losing his breakfast to appreciate the view or new information. Uncle George was amazed to be up in the air and thoroughly enjoyed the ride. How modern the world was becoming. After ten minutes they descended and John Michael could not have jumped out of the basket any faster. He sat on the grass in appreciation of returning to the earth. Miranda was not surprised to see him air sick. If he was on a swing it usually made him dizzy.

They made plans to meet up there with Butterbean tomorrow and began their walk home. Uncle Charles stayed to set the leg of the blacksmith. He was the last person you would think of to be afraid of a balloon ride that was tethered to the ground, but he was terrified and jumped out of the basket as it ascended. Some joked that he had called out to his mama. Anyway, he landed badly although in hindsight falling and breaking the picnic table probably saved his life as it broke his fall. The town was going to make him pay for that damage. He would not be shoeing horses or repairing wagon wheels any time soon. His wife was fit to be tied. She had told that fool not to waste money on that ride.

Miranda began to bring together what they would need when confronted with the dark one After hearing about the death of the Lynch family it was agreed that some outside force, perhaps a demon, had been summoned by Dr. Lynch. So they now knew he had come over 100 years before. So the question was why was he back? Had someone else summoned him? She could see now that the graves had been a part of the ceremony. She now realized why the lost ghosts could not find their graves. The markers only had been moved. That was why they could not rest.

Mama Lucy seemed to be more animated then usual as she began to brew the new potion. She had been at it for the last five days and was beginning wear down, This was of no importance to her. She had seen her death years before and accepted her fate. She added a bit of sugarcane to combat the bitter of the taste. This brew was to be eaten by all who would need protection when confronting the demon. She placed it into a pan which she sat on the hot embers in the fire. There it would stay until she deemed it ready. There was a rhythm in the making which had to be followed to make it strong. As the loaf made a crust it was branded with the ancient symbol of the earth. This was the mark of ritual food. She recited the incantation of power and displayed the movements of request. Removing it from the fire she sprinkled a touch of salt to tie it to the earth. The biggest danger was to be taken up into the swirling mass of darkness. This was to be feared more than death itself. She was done. The only thing left to do was to pray. Aunt

Eloise was very concerned about the health of Mama Lucy. She had become so pale within her darkness. Miranda was surprised to realize that the angry spirit man was at her window just waving as if he were in a parade. It was obvious he had never waved before, "You cannot back out of your agreement with your grandson" she hollered at him towards the window. As luck would have it her aunt was stepping into the room. "Young lady, that is no way to speak to any one, even a ghost. You are supposed to be a lady. Not one of those thimble ladies who work downtown." Miranda could not get over this rebuke even though she agreed a young lady did not holler at anyone. Those thimble ladies had been run out of town a few years back. When men were walking on a certain side street in the evening women would tap on a store front window with a thimble on their finger. This was how they identified themselves as ladies of the night. Nothing more needs to be said about that. Leaping from her chair and striding to the window she said, "Please stop waving. I have not seen you since the night I tried to get you to leave. What is it you want?" "I have enjoyed seeing the life in my grandson, I realize I had never lived when I was alive. This I owe to you. I have seen the coming of the dark one. I know when he will return." Looking at him she said, "If we are to be friends I should know your Christian name." "They called me Augustus when I lived", He then told her what he knew and they prepared for the day.

NYBBAS

They met Cookie when they were investigating the park the next day. Miranda was focused on speaking with the dead whose graves had not been removed. She laid on the grass and called out to any ghost who might be about. John Michael had returned to where he found the spice safe to see what else was there. They were both trying to determine how many graves remained and why only some were removed. Cookie was nothing more than a man who weighted 375 pounds. His mental capacity was less than others but he was a pure soul who befriended everyone. He had gotten his nick name from his love of sugar. John Michael enjoyed Cookie. His thought were simple and direct. He spent most of his days in the park. He was at ease out of doors and had a fear of being confined. He could not process crowds so he would avoid them.

Cookie lived with his mother who took in laundry. He often spoke with the dead in those graves as if they were alive. To him there was no difference. He just could not understand the people he saw and spoke with were dead. Meanwhile Miranda was not connecting with anyone. She thought this was a dead zone. No pun intended. Butterbean was also in the park watching the twins. They had voiced their opinion about the site. He was not sure what to think. He did give notice that Cookie was talking to someone who was not there. Taking note of this Miranda arose and walked to the side of Cookie as he was addressing the spirit. He said, "Olivia, this is Miranda. She is hunting something. She is smart." Olivia was well aware who Miranda was. She and others had been watching her from afar, They had been deceased for quite some time and had been violently disturbed in the past. They were not anxious to be disturbed again. Miranda was aware of her unease and spoke quietly. "Olivia, I sense your reluctance to make yourself known to me. I have no wish to disturb your resting place. I just need to know why these graves were defiled." Olivia gave that a long thought. Cookie had walked away to see what John Michael had found. It was a coin dated 1808. There were several others which appeared broken. Olivia finally spoke and showed herself to Miranda. "I will show you images of what occurred," Miranda knew this would drain her of energy so she sat on the grass and waited. Thinking where to begin she showed an overgrown and abandoned cemetery. This was how it looked when Dr. Lynch arrived and purchased the town and a large tract of land. This was just a decade or two after the country was formed. She had the image of him walking through the graves with a triangle in his outstretched hands, She could almost hear his jubilation of joy. This is the place he had sought. Graves within a natural triangle. He wasted no time in the removal. All tombstones where moved to the Methodist church. The workmen did not bother with placement. The graves which were moved were for show. The few villagers were told all had been moved. That was not so. Dr. Lynch had come for the sole purpose of building his home on the top of graves in order to use that power. He thought himself a god and intended to become immortal along with his entire family. Miranda was taken aback by what she saw. This was such an evil. She had asked to see and see she would. Olivia had no intention to revisit that horror again. Suddenly a massive home was covering the graves. The sky had turned dark and a swirling mass was headed for the home. There could be heard a chanting which was increasing in volume. The mass was coming down. Darkness and silence. Olivia withdrew and Miranda found herself sitting in sunshine by the river bank. She felt her heart trying to race away. She was flushed and breathing heavy. Closing her eyes she began to relax. She was surprised but appreciative of what she had witnessed. Some stuff you just cannot make up. This was the site to confront the dark one. She would have liked to have seen inside the home as the demon arrived. Olivia told her that would never be. Just to see that memory was a danger to the living. Some demon of hell had found an opportunity to manifest itself in the town in the past which gave it the opportunity to do so in the present. John Michael started to see visions in his protective spells.

The triangle symbol kept reappearing to him. Lilith told them where her books of power could be found behind the bookcase in her old bedroom. Yes, there was confidence it could be defeated. They needed the true name of this darkness in order to have some control. This dark thing was more likely than not from a region of hell. Mama Lucy walked into the house which was a rare thing for her. She had last been there when Lilith was buried all those years ago. Walking into the room perched on her old wooden cane she seemed as if she could see. Calling out to Susie she said in a hoarse and gut wrenching tone, "Nybbas has come!" This was spoken almost as a command for all to hear. Jumping up John Michael and Miranda both raced and caught her before she struck the floor. She was limp and not responsive. John Michael picked her body up and placed her on the settee. He was somewhat taken aback that she weighted next to nothing. That is when he realized she was essentially nothing more than a pile of bones held together by life. He saw that only her strong will was keeping her alive.

Aunt Eloise had Miranda to go fetch Uncle Charles. Within a moment he was in the parlor checking her pulse and listening to the flickers of her heart. A cool cloth on her forehead brought her around. "Why in the world did you walk all the way over her. That is just sapping what little strength you have." said Eloise. "Oh hush child, I am old and not afraid of death. That is the end of all. I have to tell you while it is fresh in my mind. I was making a potion to find the name of the dark one who killed at the revival. I had forgotten parts of the ritual. When the dark one came and I commanded to know his name he but laughed at me. That made me angry and I hit the pot with my hand. That gave him the moment he needed to touch me with the darkness. I awoke when I called out the name. Please tell me you heard for I no longer recall. With that she went into a sleep which lasted two days. She suddenly looked her age. Her wrinkles were dark and long. You could see her life written there."

Miranda went straight to the book of The Four Elements to see if the name was there. The name was found in a foot note. This was an obscure demon from one of the upper galleries of hell. He did not appear to be much of a demon. He had no legions that he controlled and was considered nothing more than a joke, a buffoon. Scratching his head John Michael could not make heads nor tails of this discovery. It was one thing to battle a dark force. It was another to battle one nobody even knew about. It was almost a non event. Looking his way Miranda began to put the pieces together. She realized they could walk to the three main churches in the same number of steps. Why was that she wondered? The Methodist church was in the bottom land by the woods. The Baptist church was on a very slight rise and the Catholic Church was between the two. Well that was incorrect. You could walk a straight line from one to the other but you could not walk by one when seeking the other. In other words, they were all built by the three points of an Equilateral triangle. John Michael looked up and Miranda said, "All sides are equal from point to point." "Well I certainly knew that," he replied, but Miranda knew different. She was a girl who could do math.

They were up the next few days to find a way to control Nybbas. But about this time it was learned the dead man at the entrance to the revival tent had been a priest the church had excommunicated for his beliefs. He was though to be too familiar with the evil dead. In reality he had been able to confront and evict those possessing a dark power whether they had been human or not. He had been warned in his dreams to stay away. Yet he came as he felt he knew more of this evil. He had been sure it was just a dark shadow and not a demon. He was caught unawares and died for his lack of knowledge. Aunt Eloise was pleased to received a note from the priest at the Catholic Church. He wrote, "I hope I was not abrupt when speaking of Dr. Lynch. I have prayed about this and offer my help if any help is needed. I too have a sense of evil blowing this way."

CONFRONTATION

They awoke to strong winds on that day the rain fell in waves. There was a hurricane approaching the gulf but they were not aware of that. Three days earlier the town had been covered in a reddish dust, The paper said it was from an eruption half the world away, With the rain it gave the appearance of blood washing through the streets. Yesterday ravens had been seen in a circle above the town. Folklore was that ravens were the souls of evil men, Reverend Fletcher was sure some heathen child had played that prank. He just could not figure out how that was done.

Uncle Charles looked out the window and dreaded what he saw, For the first time ever he was a witness to the dead. It was as if everyone who had ever died in the community were there. They were lining the streets and waiting, They presented themselves as faces in orbs. The dark shadows were in the distance in their familiar shapes. Without thinking he called out to his wife to look outside. She pulled back the drapery and dropped like a rock. In a moment she awoke from the faint and laughed hysterically for the next half hour. The twins were sympathetic for her but a good laugh was hard to find. They giggled as long as she laughed. They were helpless in their laughter. Even Uncle Charles was biting his lower lip. This was human nature. She finally went to sleep on the settee with the help of medication, It never hurts to wed a doctor. Mama Lucy came in and placed the loaf of protection in the center of the dining room table. She lit the candles on either side and placed the copper knife to the left. Turning her back to the table and raising her arms up to the heavens she said, "It is the time to begin as the clock strikes three." Miranda stopped wringing her hands, wiped them on her dress and came forward. She swallowed and circled the table clock wise. John Michael took his hands out of his pockets and approached Miranda. Taking her left hand they walked around the table twice more. He placed the wooden triangle beneath the loaf. Miranda had the knife in her hand and cut the loaf into triangle shapes from left to right. She was the first to partake of the bread. John Michael was the next to eat followed by Mama Lucy. Their aunt and uncle also partook even though they were not expected to confront the evil one. The loaf would keep them from being possessed. In hindsight they should have given the sixth and last piece to another. But such is life. You plan and hope for the best and then deal with what you have. The winds had calmed and the downpour turned into a shower. Miranda was watching Lilith sitting in the mirror with the cat when the chief knocked on the door. These seasoned ghost hunters jumped as one. There was flooding in the park and coffins were coming out of the earth. He had difficulty with that as he was not aware the park was a grave site. He could not understand what was happening. He needed the doc to act as a coroner. They left.

Miss Holloway appeared on the porch calling for Miranda. Her grave had popped up and she was just beside herself. It had bumped into the coffin of her mother whom she had been avoiding these past years. She had come here to hide. Miranda had no time for this foolish behavior. Especially today of all days. She could see her screaming mother coming her way. With a weary look she allowed her in. She immediately told her to stay quiet and keep out of the way. She went to the window to speak with Lilith.

Aunt Eloise was eating her piece of protection and asking why they could suddenly see the dead. To this Miranda replied, "I am not sure. It could be that the spells and incantations which guard everyone in this house have reached a saturation level." Between John Michael, myself and Mama Lucy each doing what we think is best has touched you and Uncle Charles. Think of it as a cup that cannot hold any more liquid. It overflows and covers the table. The psychic protection overwhelms the senses. In this case you can see the dead. It should not last long. This does show how strong our protective rituals are. John Michael was anxious to get to the park to check the condition of the grounds. If it is flooded or unstable they will need an alternate site. Was he afraid? Yes, a little bit. As long as the corpses remained in the ground he would be okay. It was around four when they approached the park. The twins thought there must have been at least twenty coffins sticking out of the ground. Men with frowns and concerned looks were placing them in rows. A few were hunting their shoes which came off in the mud and clay. They would have to wait for the ground to dry before placing them back into the ground. it was almost impossible to walk on that soggy ground. The only area with any firmness was the site of the revival. This was a slight rise in the ground. The large canvas tent had yet to be taken down. The workmen were afraid of the site. Most refused to even enter the tent. They had removed the bodies of the dead a few days before. The catholic priest had come to bless the site and had been seen leaving abruptly. One workman had said it looked as if the devil himself was after him. The twins waved to their uncle as they entered the tent. He and the chief were examining the coffins in the field. The chief of police believed only in what he could see. So when he stepped into the park that day with Dr. Charles and found those coffins arranged in triangles he had no explanation. The workmen had come to move them to the Baptist Cemetery. When the first coffin was placed into the wagon the team of horses could not be controlled. They broke loose and galloped away as the coffin slammed onto the ground and splintered. The wood was old, rotten and wet. The contents were strewn about. It was a headless corpse wrapped in a rotten funeral shroud. There was a bare odor of earth. Cautiously they began to look for the skull. It was not to be found. They attempted to load more wagons with no result. The horses were stressed with fear as they bucked. They were sent back to the stables. Butterbean had been watching this from a distance. He had seen his father bringing in dirt from the graveyard. His behavior was strange and both he and his wife had a rash. Butterbean had not partaken of the communion bread as it looked sour to him. That was his saving grace.

The twins could smell the death that penetrated the tent. The benches were shoved about from the removal of the corpses. The ground still held the blood of the banker. Someone had attempted to cover it with sand, Miranda was checking out the stage and noticed it had been partially dismantled in the back. For whatever reason the men had been spooked and fled the scene. Hammers and other tools were still there. Uncle Charles came in to check on the twins, John Michael was looking at the canvas walls and thought he saw an image of a face, He lit a lantern which he held up above his head, He still could not see for sure. Taking the light he began to walk around the tent when he heard the scream. It was Miranda and he had never head a scream such as that. Racing back inside he saw her staring at her face which was drawn on the wall in a massive size. The chief ran up and took the lantern as he walked all around the tent. They could see images of Mama Lucy cut in half, Uncle Charles and Aunt Eloise as bloodied and dead. At the very top of the tent was an image of Lilith. She was disfigured and has a look of terror on her face. The images were too horrid to view. This had drained their energy and spirit. They crawled in the carriage and were asleep by the time they arrived home. They slept in their clothes that night as Mama Lucy took in this new information. She called for Lilith and they planned for the part they would play. The child would need help to survive the following day. She called out to those who could help. There were two who she had to have for any hope of the survival of the twins. It was now obvious what the darkness wanted. To feed on the gifts of the children. The following morning was curious in that the ravens were a black mass in the distance. There was a stillness in the air which had not been seen since creation. No wind, not even a breeze. The dogs and cats and even the hens made no sound. Anyone walking in the street only heard the echoes of their own footsteps. Children were not seen nor heard. The grip of fear was about to descend. The angry man, Augustus, was seen pacing his yard in a rhythmic manner. Miss Holloway had spoken to Lilith and conferred with Mama Lucy. The social circle of the dead were talking among themselves under that Magnolia tree. It appeared that most of the spirits knew a darkness was fast approaching. Mr. Blessing recalled many ghosts who had been consumed by the dark ones. Why that Martha Green had just been consumed. That had always been a danger in being a ghost. He knew what a stronger dark shadow could do. His one fear was in any dark shadow absorbing a spirit that had seen the light. If this happened than the dark could not be defeated. Lilith was one such spirit. Therefore she was a target for the darkness. Even more than the twins. Butterbean ran up the flew blocks and was passing under that Magnolia tree. He noted the leaves rustling without the benefit of wind. As he jumped onto the porch there was a strong feeling of being watched. The hair on the back of his neck was raised and a chill had crossed his body. Aunt Eloise came to the door looking pale and with a tired walk. The twins had a weary look but were full of energy. He told them what he had seen his father do at the graveyard. Miranda stood up along with her brother. Both took a deep breath and kissed the other to bind their spirits together. Yes, they felt the power of this darkness and realized it was time. Aunt Eloise told them to wait until their uncle could harness the wagon. They felt a presence in the room and turned as if on cue to see Mama Lucy. Dressed in layers of white and beige she represented and involved the purity of life as a power. Looking at Eloise she spoke in a strong and commanding voice. "Let the children go. It is their time." Aunt Eloise sat in the chair and began to disagree. "Hush woman," said Mama Lucy. "The twins have something to control. This is their time. This is why they are. It is not for you nor me to interfere." As she left the room she turned back and said, "As you begin your walk look about." Then she was gone.

Butterbean just said "Whoa" as they left the house. He was walking so close to the twins that they gave the appearance of being a three headed entity. That boy was scared. Now I do not mean scared as if your dad found out what you did last week. I am talking so scared you run home, lock your door and hide up under your bed. They passed the square and there was the old soldier saluting the twins. Now this simple gesture of respect rebuilt their confidence. Often the views of others let's you know you are valuable and on the right path. This can be a source of strength and so it was. Many of the dead were following the children for that sense of protection they felt around them. They saw the cats and knew what they were. The twins were so focused on the task at hand that they had forgotten about the protectors. It was Mama Lucy that had sent them on their way. Mama Lucy looked weary as she sent off the twins. Aunt Eloise was beyond herself with worry. Uncle Charles had seen more than he ever imagined during the past few days. He was about to go and find the twins but Mama Lucy stopped him. He would be no good to anyone if he did not survive the night. All he would be was a target. Lilith had gone to her grave to recover her strength and focus on the battle to come. Naturally the cat was with her and sat atop the tomb. Meanwhile Mama Lucy was preparing for what she was about to do. She stepped into the yard and collected the pine sap from the tree she had tapped. This was placed in a mason jar with some holy water and shaken lightly as she muttered a few sacred words. Calling out for Uncle Charles to harness the buggy she returned to the house. There was something to do and now was the time to leave. Why did time always seem to move so quickly? She was saying a prayer as they left the house. The children turned into the churchyard and circled the small church. Miranda was drawn to the stained glass window which had blown out in back of the altar. The shattered glass was covering the ground. The oddest thing was the glass all seemed to be in triangles. John Micheal could sense the dark power that had shattered the window. The ghosts of the Vaxley children were in the courtyard watching the dark ones emerging from the paths leading into and from the forest. Some were human forms but most were creatures unknown in the light of day. A few with elongated torsos and limbs were clinging to the outside of the church. Chaos was coming and they sensed this is where the dark one would emerge. John Michael recited a chant in an attempt to seal this perceived gate. He knew it was too little and far too late. They had missed that opportunity. The ghost children had told them of the path and they had failed to address it at that time. They had missed the significance. It was much more than a way station for the dead. It was a vortex of energy by which evil could emerge. This could prove to be their undoing. The cats raced to the church and jumped onto the creature hanging from the church. There was a screech and the creature was gone. The cats were stretching and licking their lips. They were looking forward to the main course and walked through the graves and nibbled on other pieces of darkness. Everyone likes an appetizer. Augustus, once the angry man, did not believe in a god. He thought death was a natural thing and was not directed by any entity. He had no time for the Bible pushers. Death had yet to change his mind. Now mind you, he did believe there was a supernatural world. That was where his consciousness survived. He just did not believe any entity directed the paths taken. He coincided if the dark force turned out to be a demon from hell then he would have to rethink his views. To him it was strange that most Christians did not believe in the supernatural. How did they explain the holy ghost? He was mulling this over as he followed the twins. He was not comfortable leaving his house. This he did out of respect and fear for the twins. He felt a debt to them. That was way he was in the lead with the spirits, Miss Holloway was right there in front too. She was going to protect her friend. Truth be known she was a bit interested in Augustus. True, she was from an earlier time but they were near the same age at their death. They resumed their walk to the park. There was now such a large number of the dead above their heads that they could not be counted. The protectors were now leading the way. Everyone was feeding off the energy from the dead. Then came the sound and the darker darkness. The dark one had come through the path by the Methodist Church. From behind they could sense it coming. It seemed to envelope the town as it journeyed to the park. There was a slight quiver of the ground and a slap of thunder caused by the heat of the night. They now knew it was there, waiting in anticipation. They continued to walk towards the park. No one appeared on the street. The churches were full of those who were frighted by the recent events and they were at prayer for the safety of them and the town. The Catholic priest had begun to perform a high mass yesterday and expected to continue throughout the night. He had unloaded bags of salt all around the tomb of the Lynch family, He was taking no chances and had the permission of the bishop for the old rituals he had performed.

The closer they approached the darkness the heavier the air became. They could see the dark shadows surrounding the park at the edges of the triangle. As they approached the shadows parted. The shadows were so strong that even Butterbean observed them. There must have been hundreds of all shapes and levels of darkness. His eyes were so big as his mouth hung open that both the twins had the giggles. You could sense the easing of their minds which allowed them to focus. It was noted the shadows retreated a bit at this time. They sensed a touch of power there. Miranda looked at her brother and said, "Do not engage the dark one. My focus will only be directed on the entity. If I fail look away or we both will be taken into the void." Showing his love for his sibling he replied, "I will not let you go alone into the darkness. We are and have always been one." With tears in their eyes they entered the tent as Butterbean swept aside the dead ravens which surrounded the tent. The benches were arranged in a circle with a large space in the center. The stage was nothing more than a mass of splinters. Butterbean was surprised to see his father standing there. He made note of the rash covering his head. It seemed to have a life of its own as it crawled up and around the face. There was an odor of something he had never smelled. Like an odor of nothing but fear. Next he noted the figures surrounding him. They were all members of their church. They were followers of John Wesley and not of this darkness. Butterbean did not understand until Miranda said, "they are all affected with the evil. Can you not see their rashes or whatever it is crawling over their bodies." That was when he realized even his mother was there. How had her goodness been corrupted? He could see she looked unfocused. Not unlike puppets in a show. Could they be saved? All these thoughts were crowding his head as the twins drew a triangle around him on the ground. He had been attempting to engage his mother who could only look ahead. He was told not to leave the triangle and not to address the entity. Bending down the twins each drew a triangle in the sand and stood on either side and a little in front of Butterbean. They invoked the ritual of protection and true sight. The air became even more dense as the congregation stood and sang of the glories of hell. Reverend Fletcher had a solo as he sang along with a look of crazy evil all about his face. He stepped back as he gave the floor to Nybbas who suddenly appeared within the circle. Tipping his hat to the children he grinned and opened the horror of his mouth. Inside were the damned which gave him power and substance. The pause was unbearable and then he spoke. Miranda was invoking the faith of St. Margaret and clasping her metal so hard her hand began to bleed. John Michael was moving the metal of St. David hand to hand in a nervous gesture. Butterbean sat within his triangle as he feared stepping out in error. He figured this was the safest thing to do. He was almost too scared to breathe.

The congregation began to chant as they walked around the dark form. He had expected the twins to cave in to his strength. He had confronted the 66 members of the Lynch family with ease. They capitulated within a moment of his arrival. Just his presence was enough to corrupt most environments. These children were much stronger and focused. They were surrounded by the power of good. Miranda was seeing the horrorsof the third level of hell as was her brother. Both continued to chant. The demon was impatient and began to growl. He expected light residence. These were mere children. He had not thought of them as a force to struggle with. To be restricted from his goal fed his anger. The town was ripe to be taken into the darkness. What a triumph he would have in hell. They would never call him a charlatan again. His vanity would be his undoing. Dropping his elongated arms into the ground he dug up the earth as he called for the dead to arise and assist him. The remaining coffins rose from the ground. The figures within them set up an fell apart. These grave were very old and no longer held anything of substance. Even the evil one was unable to bind them together for his cause. The ravens were summoned by the dark one. The flock descended and encircled the demon in a swirling mass which appeared to give him some strength. Butterbean was resisting the urge to step outside of the triangle. He had become disoriented, confused and too scared to even think. His dad was calling out to him as the congregation began to sway about Nybbas. This dark one could not break the protective triangles. Turning all his focus towards the little friend of the twins he called him forward. Butterbean fell out of the triangle and was immediately possessed by the demon. He began to speak as Nybbas. "I am older than the earth and younger that the stars and yet you mock me. You are but a mortal whose life is but a moment in time. And yet you resist me. I was a witness to the angels as they fell away from God. Still you rebuke me." Miranda had been listening to these words coming from the mouth of her friend. She could see the horror that was felt as he was controlled by the demon. Why had they not thought to offer a piece of that bread of protection to him? Speaking directly to the demon she asked. "What do you require in this realm?" With a smirk he replied, "why girl I came for you and yours. The power you hold is wanted by many. You are but a source of power and your brother extends that energy. We have not seen your kind since the templar knights fought in the holy land." The demon began to elongate and soon filled the tent as he loomed over the children. John Michael reached into his back pocket and threw out two triangles which were blessed by the church. One of iron and the other of copper. The iron was to root the demon to the ground and the copper was to dispel his energy. There was a crackling sound as the demon seemed to react to the metals. The protectors leaped onto the darkness and were thrown off but they could sense a weakness in the mass. Miranda was praying for the intervention of St. Margaret and all the saints she could name. For a moment John Michael thought he saw the image of St David wearing his crown as king and holding the cross of salvation, This gave him the strength he needed to continue. Suddenly Augustus and Miss Holloway were leading an enormous band of spirits who were diving at the darkness of this demon. This made the demon more angry and then the protectors returned to the fight. Lilith joined Miranda in the circle and their powers grew. One of the protectors John Michael had nicknamed Hell Cat scratched Butterbean releasing him of his possession by Nybbas. The cats were biting and scratching the congregation releasing many who were so scared and confused as they fled the tent. The images on the canvas tent seemed to grow and move. You could smell the sulfur as the evil grew. The twins were calling for this demon to return to hell where he was nothing but a minor player. The air was thick with this darkness and then Mama Lucy was at the door. She was in all her glory as she entered the space. Turning her way the demon laughed and laughed again. "Old woman, you could not defeat me in your day and that has been long past," he said as he snickered to show his disdain. Looking at him without a trace of fear and with all the power she could muster she replied, "I am not here to defeat you. I have come to send you back to hell where you have no hope, only desire for what you can never have. Dr. Lynch summoned you to his sorrow. We did not ask for you nor do we want you. We reject you, You have no power here." The twins stepped out of the triangle of protection and stood to either side of Mama Lucy. Butterbean and his dad stood behind the three. The protectors were now at the front of the three. As the demon pointed towards them Mama Lucy withdrew a silver hand mirror and chanted, "look at your darkness, turn away from we. Get yourself back to hell where you need to be." This they repeated four times as she tossed the bottle of tar water at his feet and it broke open splattering his form. His rage was taken up with the wind inside the tent. The ravens were dead and falling from the sky. They covered their ears from the sound of his wail. It was like listening to the sorrow of all the lost souls who were beyond redemption. His form began to drip like candle wax as it puddled on the ground. Taking a last long look at the demon Mama Lucy screamed, "get yourself back to hell". The face of the demon crowded the space and then became nothing more than a black hole. Silence. Stillness. They collapsed from exhaustion. Suddenly the tent was filled with lightening bugs which totally dispelled the darkness. They had won. Aunt Eloise and Uncle Charles rushed into the tent. The twins were crying as they cradled Mama Lucy in their arms. It was her time and she was gone. The twins watched as her spirit went into the light. Lilith was at her side as was that cat. The funeral was a private affair. Just the family and spirits were in attendance as homage was given to this great lady. She was embarrassed by this praise as she sat with the children and Lilith. As they returned to the house children were jumping rope in the street. Their chant already spoke of the victory. "When the earth has turned red and the ravens are dead, that is when the town will again be well." This is all I have to say about my grandmother and her twin. She and Lilith still come to visit. And yes, that old cat often tags along.